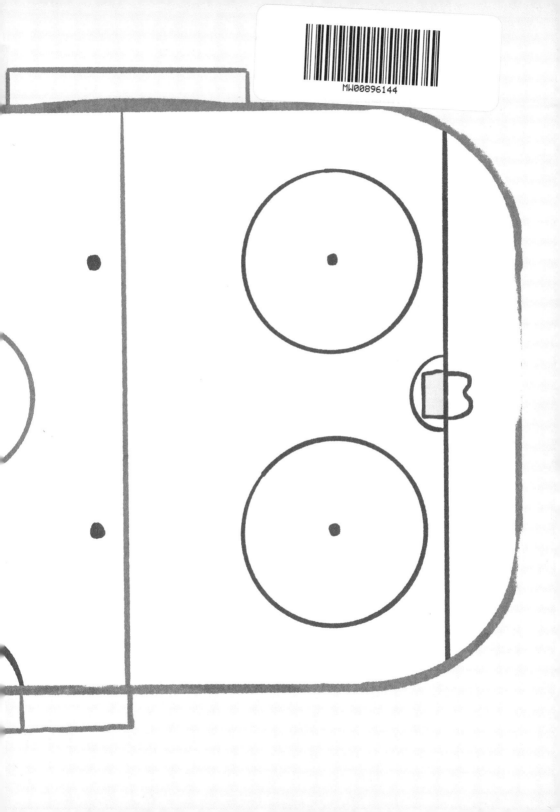

This book series is special to our family. The books teach real life lessons and the joys of hockey, family, and teammates. Hockey Day is a special holiday to all of us in Minnesota. We love these books!

—*Matt and Bridget Cullen*
Three-time Stanley Cup champion

I'm a big fan of books that teach kids about hockey and more importantly about the value of accepting those who may be different and working together as a team. It's important to lead by example and treat everyone with the same respect.

—*Claude Giroux*
Captain, Philadelphia Flyers

Keep reading, keep skating, and keep making new friends. That's what life is all about.

—*Rick Nash*
Former NHL player, Boston Bruins

This book has great lessons kids everywhere! I'm so happy my good friend Ann and the American Special Hockey Association can be an inspiration for so many people!

—*Alex Ovechkin*
Captain, Washington Capitals

This book teaches real life lessons through sport, through victory and losses, and emphasizes the importance of hard work regardless of score.

—*Jocelyne Nicole Lamoureux-Davidson*
Olympic gold medalist, Team USA

A fun story that shares the love of family and hockey!

—*Corey Perry*
NHL All-Star, Dallas Stars

Like all Minnesotans, we vote yes for Hockey Day and treasure the friendships hockey gives to all players! Keep reading!

—*Phil and Sen. Karin Housley*
Hockey Hall of Famer

I might dye my beard red, white, and blue for special hockey! Special hockey rocks! Reading is important! Do it!

—*Brent Burns*
Defenseman, San Jose Sharks

It's super cool playing hockey with my friends. I love skating, meeting new friends, and cheering for the Caps! A book about hockey, the Ice Dogs, and my dream of being the Capitals announcer is a hat trick of awesomeness!

—*Ann Schaab*
Washington Ice Dogs

I love the way this book celebrates individual differences, strengths, and similarities. When children learn about themselves, others, and the world around them, that is the ultimate hat trick.

—*Aimee Jordan*
Lila's mom; advocate for people with disabilities

Hockey is more than a sport—it's a culture. And the best part of hockey's culture is that it continually brings friends together.

—*Avery Hakstol*
Daughter of NHL coach Dave and Erinn Hakstol

HOCKEY EVERYDAY, EVERY WAY

JAYNE J. JONES BEEHLER

ILLUSTRATED BY CORY JONES

Whitaker
Playhouse

HOCKEY EVERY DAY, EVERY WAY

ISBN: 978-1-64123-666-9
eBook ISBN: 978-1-64123-776-5
Printed in the United States of America

Illustrated by Cory Jones

Whitaker House
1030 Hunt Valley Circle
New Kensington, PA 15068
www.whitakerhouse.com

1 2 3 4 5 6 7 8 9 10 11 ⨆ 28 27 26 25 24 23 22 21

DEDICATION

For the joys of hockey that inspire us all.

A NOTE FROM JAYNE

The Drop the Puck series, showcasing brothers Blaine and Cullen, continues with this third tale. Ann and Blaine were born with Down syndrome and have special needs. Down syndrome is a genetic disorder that can cause physical growth delays, characteristic facial features, and mild to moderate intellectual disability. Blaine's speech at times can be stuttering, slurring, and repetitive.

This tale introduces Lila, inspired by our friend who is a happy, spirited reader of the series and a new hockey player. Lila was born with cerebral palsy, or CP. CP is a permanent movement disorder that stiffens muscles and makes for poor coordination. However, in Lila's honor, we use the term *CP* to stand for *competitive player*. Lila is one of the fastest skaters on the ice.

The illustrations in *Hockey Every Day, Every Way* are inspired by real photos, stories, and inspirational people. Grab your skates—it's time to play!

LILA'S NEW HOME: HOCKEYTOWN USA

"Will hockey practice be canceled tonight because of the blizzard?" Lila asked.

"Not a chance—not in Hockeytown USA!" her mom replied with a laugh.

As the snow piled high, Lila and her family were enjoying their second full week in their new hometown. Lila was excited to practice with the Minnesota Bears, her new special hockey team. "Yesterday at school, Blaine asked if we could snap cross-country skis onto my wheelchair!" she said, giggling.

"You'd certainly get across town faster that way," her dad replied, giving Lila's chair a playful push before pulling her back into place.

9

"Just like on the ice." A dreamy look passed over Lila's face, the homework in her lap forgotten.

"Does Blaine skate?" her mom asked.

"Does it snow in Minne-snow-ta?" Lila joked.

"Good point!" her mom said, smiling.

After a few moments, Lila's face became serious. "I'm not sure what's harder: moving to a new school or joining a new hockey team. I'll miss skating with Jason and Carly at practices." Lila's big eyes filled with tears.

"Whoa, whoa, whoa," her dad said. "Don't forget, Hockeytown USA has lots of Olympians and professional players who skate with the Bears."

"Jason helped me skate super fast!" said Lila, brightening. "Almost faster than him!"

"And now you'll be able to put those skills to good use," said her dad, ruffling her hair.

The family shared a smile as Lila's mom hugged her. "You've done great!" she said. "I'm proud of you. Keeping up with your reading and math, making all your new friends, and playing for the Minnesota Bears!"

"A superb list of accomplishments for just two weeks! I can't wait to see you in a Bears jersey for your first game! Can I hiss every time you score?" her dad asked.

"Bears don't hiss!" Lila said with a snort.

"From the day you were born, you have been the queen of grit and determination, Miss Lila," her mom proclaimed. "Nothing stands in your way."

"Not even fifteen inches of fresh snow," said her dad, gesturing at the drifts piling up outside. "Grab those cross-country skis, and let's go to hockey practice!"

Lila whooped and put her homework aside. "Wheels up! Skates on!" The saying had become the family's personal motto.

"Wow! They've already plowed it!" Lila's dad said as he pulled the family van into the arena's parking lot. Patches of white showed here and there, but it was mostly a freshly cleared path for Lila's wheelchair to drive on.

"I'm a little nervous," Lila told her mom as they headed inside.

"It's your second practice with the Bears," her mom replied, reaching down to take her daughter's hand. "Of course, you're nervous. But the Lila I know is the queen of—"

"Grit and determination," Lila interrupted, her voice a little sarcastic. She'd heard the phrase a lot.

As the family walked into the arena's waiting room, Avery ran up to Lila, greeting her with a hug. "You made it!"

"What are you doing here?" Lila asked Avery.

"You silly goose! We help with practice! Luke, Cullen, Paisley, and, of course, Blaine and Ann!" Avery answered as the other kids filed into the waiting room, waving to Lila and her family.

"It's my favorite practice of the week!" Paisley chimed in, brandishing her hockey stick enthusiastically.

"And soon to be our favorite practice too!" Lila's dad replied with a laugh.

"Right on!" Luke hollered from afar.

"Ddddiiiiddd you skkiiii here?" Blaine asked Lila, pointing at the snow that still clung to the edges of her wheels. They both laughed.

13

"Listen up, everyone!" Cullen announced as he laced up his skates. "There's no need for anyone to rush home after today's practice to spend countless hours priming and stewing over your Valentine's Day mailbox. I've got the all-school first-place ribbon in the bag!"

"Hardy-har-har!" Avery mouthed to the others. "I've been working all weekend on my mailbox," she announced. "It's sparkly glam meets Lamoureux!"

"Don't count on that ribbon just yet! My dad and I have a graduate degree in papier-mâché! We're pasting and playing to win!" Paisley said with a mischievous grin.

"I'm taking a year off from my traditional hockey theme," said Luke. Everyone looked stunned.

"Not me! The first-place ribbon will be for my shrine to the Great One!" Cullen announced, standing up with his skates on and posing like a champion.

"IIIIIII stttillll neeedddd to maaakkkee minne," said Blaine.

"Me too!" Lila anxiously looked at her parents, then back at the other kids. "You make Valentine's Day mailboxes for school?"

"We sure do! Here in Hockeytown, it's a big deal. We love it!" Paisley told her.

"We bring a Valentine for everyone in our school!" Luke chimed in.

"Everyone?" asked Lila.

"Yes, we're a small town with a whole lot of heart!" Avery replied. "And a love of competition," she added, rolling her eyes at Cullen.

"Teeaacchers gettt them too!" Blaine told Lila.

Lila hadn't known about this all-school competition, and Valentine's Day was just four days away. Her little heart thumped faster and louder.

As Lila's dad helped tie her skates, he told her with a wink, "Don't worry—that first-place ribbon will be ours."

"Thanks, Dad! Wheels up! Skates on!" Lila said before shooting out onto the ice.

The warmth of small-town traditions and friendships made Hockeytown USA the true Great One.

2

JUST GIVE ME ONE SHOT, VALENTINE!

Lila's mom and dad brainstormed Valentine's Day ideas through the entire Minnesota Bears practice.

"I can't wait to share our list with Lila," her mom said, pausing to cheer as her daughter slapped the puck into the net. "I hope playing hockey eased her nerves."

"A few hiccups will always happen with a move into a new town and school," Lila's dad said, "but this is an easy one to fix!"

"That was fun!" Lila exclaimed, clambering off the ice.

"We're thrilled you had fun. That's what matters most!" said Lila's mom as she pulled off Lila's skates.

"See you tomorrow at school!" Avery called, waving to Lila.

"Great shot, Lila!" Cullen shouted as he left.

Lila cheerfully waved at the pair, but after they had gone, she sighed. "I didn't know anything about Valentine's Day. I don't want to look silly as the new kid!"

"Don't worry," her dad told her. "We already have a list of ideas!"

Back at the family home, Lila's dad grabbed the list and presented it to Lila.

Lila laughed at all the ideas. "I'm more worried about designing my mailbox!"

"I have an idea! We could have the Burlap Baker make heart hockey cookies with 'Icing isn't just for cookies' written on them and tie a card to each one!" her mom suggested.

"I can't tie ribbon very good," Lila replied, looking down at her hands, "and cutting paper is tough."

"Since when do you give up so easily?" her dad asked. "You could paint big, poster-sized sheets of paper," he said, gesturing expansively at an imaginary sheet. "After your masterpiece dries, we could hold the paper while you cut out cards with your left hand."

"What about my mailbox? They made it sound like I need an entry for an art gallery competition! I can't papier-mâché! I can't even squeeze a glue bottle with my hands like everyone else!" Lila sighed.

"We are a family and a team first. We are all in this together!" replied her dad. "If you need help with the glue, or anything else, we're there for you."

"We could make your mailbox look like a hockey palace with your name across the front," her mom suggested.

"Or we could cut tag board and make a double-sided hockey skate," her dad offered. "The card opening would be the hole in the blade!"

19

"See, Lila? There are tons of great mailbox ideas. No need for a pity party!" her mom said. "You play with Legos all the time to build mastermind creations with Le-Glue. Why can't you use Le-Glue on your mailbox?"

"If Le-Glue can fix broken hockey sticks, I think it can build your mailbox masterpiece!" said her dad.

Lila smiled. Le-Glue reminded her of her friend, Tripp Phillips, who'd invented it. She knew that he wouldn't give up, and neither would she. She started to think of her own mailbox ideas.

There were a few minutes of silence as the family mulled over additional ideas.

"I know! I know! I got it!" Lila cried, eyes sparkling. "We could make a jersey with Jason's number on it!"

"We could add, 'Score! Have a sweet Valentine's Day! Zuck-er Up!'" her mom suggested.

The family laughed.

"We have work to do! And cookies to order!" her dad exclaimed, rising to his feet.

"Wheels up! Skates on!" Lila cheered.

The baker set the box of cookies on the counter. Lila's mom peered down at them through the plastic window in the top of the box.

"They look absolutely perfect! Lila will love them!" Lila's mom said, staring at the dozens of frosted cookies.

"It was our pleasure! Frosted cookies make everyone's day— young and old!" the small-town baker replied as she pulled a fresh batch of new treats from the oven.

"It must be all the small-town magic and love that goes into them!" said Lila's mom.

"We are thrilled Lila and your family moved to Hockeytown USA," the baker told her as she handed over a receipt. "Come back anytime!"

PERIOD 1
BE MINE
4
VALENTINES

BLANE

ANN

3
HOCKEY FRIENDSHIPS

"They're so cute!" Lila said, grinning at the rows of cookies spread out in front of her. Together, her mom and dad helped Lila to tie on the last Valentine's card.

Lila's mom took a picture of her perfected jersey mailbox and a few of the cookies. She texted the picture to Jason and Carly, adding, "Your heart for special hockey runs from Hockeytown USA, through all the State of Hockey!"

Carly texted back in seconds, "Adorable! Give our girl a squeeze! Wheels up! Skates on!"

The school's hallways were jammed full of tables decorated with homemade, creative mailboxes. "I've never seen anything like this!" Lila said to Blaine.

"It'ssss sooooo cool," Blaine responded, gazing at the creations that peppered the walkway.

"Best Valentine's Day party in the state," Avery added, taking care not to knock over any boxes as she approached her friends.

The kids gathered their boxes together. Avery had made a Team USA mailbox. Paisley had made a papier-mâché scoreboard. Blaine had decorated a shoebox in a festive Valentine's Day theme. Ann's box looked like a traditional mailbox with a little red flag that went up and down. Luke had crafted a bulldog resembling his own dog, Stanley Cup.

"I think we should stick to playing hockey—these arts and crafts aren't our arena!" Paisley joked.

"Speak for yourself! My Stanley Cup is spot on!" Luke bragged.

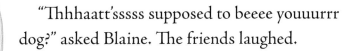

"Thhhaatt'sssss supposed to beeee youuurrr dog?" asked Blaine. The friends laughed.

"Your icing cookies are too cute to eat!" Avery told Lila.

"And so tasty!" added Ann through a mouthful of baked goods.

"Iiiiiii alreaddyyy had mmminne!" said Blaine, rubbing his stomach.

"Did you see my Great One shrine?" asked Cullen. "I just love the W. G. It's already in the hall of fame aisle."

"I did see it…but if it's so great, then where's your first-place ribbon?" Paisley asked, teasing him.

"It's on Lila's sweet jersey!" said Luke. He gave Lila a high-five.

"For real?" Lila asked, beaming.

"Yup," replied Ann, "for real!" She took Lila by the hand and guided her to see the ribbon for herself.

Some daily tasks were more challenging for Lila than others. Because of her cerebral palsy, she had a hard time with muscle tone, movements, and motor skills. At school, Lila had an aide to help her with the activities that gave her trouble.

The aide pushed Lila's wheelchair down the hall to gather her mailbox. A first-place ribbon was taped to the front. "This mailbox is so sturdy! It must be glued well," the aide said, smiling as she tapped the hard surface. "You did a great job."

"I'll need to text my friend," Lila told her. "He created Le-Glue, and he's just a kid!"

"No such thing as just a kid in my world! Just like you, the queen of grit and determination!" the aide replied.

When Lila opened her mailbox, she saw that it was full of cards, candy, and treats. She couldn't wait to show her parents. Her aide helped carry her mailbox to the school bus, making sure not to spill any of the treats.

After dinner, Lila and her parents opened every card she'd received. They cherished reading them out loud. Many were traditional greetings. More than half of them shared the town's love for hockey.

Lila found a special invite tucked into the mailbox and read it out loud, "We are wild about hockey! You are invited to my sleepover birthday party! Join us for a wild game with mini donuts and ice cream! Love, Paisley." Lila looked up at her parents, smiling. "I've never been invited for a sleepover!"

The other friends had received the same special invite. It was going to be a wonderful night!

4

REGIONALS: HATS, HARDWARE, AND SOCKS

The Hockeytown USA Pee Wees were regionally ranked as the first-place squad after their season play ended undefeated, and they were headed into regional playoffs. It was winners-only advance play through the tournament. Roseau, neighbor and rival, ranked last place. But that was before their game with Hockeytown—and they were ready to compete.

After the game, the Hockeytown team was not happy. They entered the locker room in a cloud of gloom.

"Well, that stunk!" Luke said, tossing his stick to the locker-room floor with an explosive clatter.

"One and done should be tattooed on our goalie's mask," Cullen said, unlacing his skates. They had lost 10–0.

"Did we just get ten-runned?" asked Paisley, squirting water at him.

"That's a different game," replied Luke.

"No wonder we lost." Avery shook her head.

Their coach joined the discussion. "We got outplayed, team."

"Outplayed?" Cullen scoffed. "Out of our league, blown away! We lost to the last-place team—and Roseau!"

"They'll never let us forget this," said Luke, grunting as he bent down to pick up his stick.

"Miss Marvin was even here watching!" Paisley growled in frustration. "How humiliating."

"Good teams don't let one loss crush them!" their coach shouted at them. "Good teams are humble."

"We were cocky. They were humble," said Avery. "They came ready to not only play but play to win."

"We thought we could just show up and not play as a team," admitted Luke.

"Boy, did we just learn a lesson," said Paisley. "We got creamed."

After a moment of angry silence, Cullen said, "I can't believe Will Stinson's celly after his hat trick!"

"Yeah, who acts like that? Throwing his stick in the air like a javelin!" Luke complained.

"Yoouuuuuu wouldddd, Cullennnn," replied Blaine.

"I would not."

"Yes, you would. We all would," Paisley admitted.

"Good for Will Stinson. He deserved a celebration like that!" said Avery.

"We just learned a life lesson on that rink," their coach told them. "You can hang your heads for the next six months until the puck drops again, or you can stand tall, play to your potential, and work hard. The choice is yours! You're in charge of your attitude."

The girls turned to head into their dressing room, but just then, they heard a knock on the door.

"Who knocks on a locker room door?" Avery asked.

"We don't want any. Go away," Cullen snapped.

The door swung open with a bang. "Easy!" cried Paisley, walking to greet the new arrivals.

Two of Roseau's star players, Will Stinson and Tripp Phillips, appeared.

"With a name like Tripp, I'm surprised you can skate," Luke joked. When no one else laughed, he hastily returned to packing up his gear.

"We just wanted to come and congratulate you guys on a great season," Will Stinson told them.

"That's very cool of you," said Avery as she reached forward to shake his hand. "I'm not sure we would have done the same thing."

33

"You went undefeated, and that's hard to do. We didn't even win a single game!" said Tripp.

"Those are pretty sweet socks you got on," Cullen said reluctantly, pointing to Will Stinson's colorful diamond socks.

"We all wore them today. A team that plays together, wins together," the rival player replied.

"Weeeeeeee bettttttter orrrrrrrddder sssssooooocks for nexxxtt seasssson," Blaine said. Everyone laughed and finally felt a little better.

"I know it sounds weird, but do you guys want to take a pic?" Avery asked. Cullen gave her a confused look.

"Great idea, Avery!" Paisley jumped up and gathered the team around Will and Tripp. After a lot of squeezing, they managed to fit everyone into the frame.

Posting the pic, Luke typed: "Champs on and off the ice. Cool dudes with crazy socks, hats, and hardware."

After the game, Paisley checked her phone and saw a text from Lila: "Yes! Yes! Yes! I get to come to your sleepover. I'm wild about hockey! Thanks for including me! You are the best!"

The text made Paisley smile. She ran to show her parents.

"That's what life is all about—it's the little things," her dad said.

"It's not always about winning a hockey game," her mom added. "Sometimes, losing comes with incredible moments of learning."

5

WILD ABOUT HOCKEY AND FRIENDS

"Wow, this arena is beyond awesome!" Lila exclaimed, her face glowing as she looked around the Xcel Energy Center in Saint Paul, Minnesota.

"We played here for a state tourney," Luke told her.

"This is what I call a rink!" said Avery.

"Do you smell popcorn?" Ann asked.

A powerful aroma of butter and salt hung in the air. The teammates all stared at every corner. It was unusually quiet, which added to the magical atmosphere of the arena.

"I love being friends with all of you," Lila said, breaking the silence.

"Me too!" Ann answered quickly.

"Same!" Paisley added.

"Ditto!" Luke agreed.

"Hooowww willll youuuu gettt intoooo your sssseeeatt for the gammmme?" Blaine asked.

Ann pushed him forward in embarrassment. "We don't ask that!"

"Good question, Blaine," said Paisley's dad, raising his voice to be heard above the chatter. "We have everyone sitting in Jason and Carly's suite for the game." He led them all in the direction of the suite.

The friends hurried and huddled into the arena suite.

"Fancy schmancy!" said Avery, taking in the trappings around them.

"I'd like some Grey Poupon with my hot dog," Cullen said with a British accent.

"I just want popcorn!" Ann whispered to him.

"Whoa, all-you-can-eat food!" said Luke.

"I liikkkkeee miniiii donutssss," said Blaine.

"No, you love mini donuts!" Lila corrected him.

"Yessssss, I doooooo!" replied Blaine, giving her a fist bump. Lila managed to hold her fist.

"Looks like you can have all the mini donuts you want here!" Avery said, grabbing a plate for herself.

"Until he pukes," Cullen added. "Easy on the donuts, bro. Lila, can I get you a plate?"

"Yes, that would be terrific! Can I roll my wheelchair right up to the railing to watch the game?" Lila asked.

"You betcha!" Paisley's mom answered.

"Everyone look here in 5-4-3-2-1," the cameraman yelled as the jumbotron announced a game contest. The arena roared for the fan favorite: the dance fever competition.

"I'm glad it's not the kiss cam!" Ann said, laughing.

The friends gathered close together and jumped right up. The upbeat, trendy music made it easy to bust a few fast dance moves. What the kids lacked in skill, they made up for with energy.

Avery noticed that Lila was sitting still, motionless. She turned to Cullen and winked.

Together, the duo quickly crowded around Lila's wheelchair. Lila instantly joined in the dancing, and the crowd roared even louder with cheers and applause. The jumbotron cameraman kept focused on the group. They were the highlight of the intermission break.

Ref. Riley texted Ref. Rosee, "Watching the game? We know those great kids and teammates!"

"Made my heart swell. Hockey is for everyone, every day and every way!" Ref Rosee responded.

"What section?" Jagger Stephen texted Cullen and Luke.

"What?" Cullen responded.

"What s-e-c-t-i-on?" he texted again, this time adding a photo of him and McLaren.

"No way! Are you here?" Cullen texted back. Then he read the conversation out loud so everyone knew that Jagger Stephen and McLaren had seen them dance.

"I can't believe we made national TV!" Luke shouted.

"Duh. Our dads are playing!" Jagger Stephen texted Cullen.

"Funnnnn!" Blaine cheered.

"Meet up after the game? Work on those dance moves!" McLaren sent.

"We dance and dangle on the ice, c ya after game!" Cullen replied.

"That game was fun!" Avery shouted.

"Wild for the win—McLaren and Jagger Stephen will be grouchy!" replied Cullen.

After the game, the friends got an extra-special surprise treat.

"Jason and Carly heard that Lila was coming with us today. They invited us to come to the locker room and meet the team!" Paisley's dad announced.

"What? Wait, say it again!" said Luke.

"For real? Don't joke about meeting Zucker," said Avery. "This is the best birthday sleepover ever."

"Cannnnn girrlllls go innnnn the locker rooommm?" Blaine asked, getting himself another push from Ann.

"We rule the locker room," Paisley said as she high-fived Lila.

"Yes, we do!" Ann agreed.

"Hoooowwww will Lila gettttt thereeee?" asked Blaine. Ann stared at Blaine intently and zipped her fingers across her mouth at him.

"Is there an elevator?" Lila asked.

"Of course, we have many elevators and accessible routes," an arena escort assured her.

"Cooooolllll!" said Blaine.

"Wheels up. Skates on!" Luke gestured for the friends to follow the arena escort.

6

MORE THAN A HOCKEY GAME

The elevator door opened onto the lower level. The escort pushed Lila out, and her friends nervously followed. Ahead of them, the gathering area in front of the locker room door was buzzing with people. Even Blaine was speechless at the sight of the waiting crowd.

Carly spotted Lila and came rushing toward her. She wrapped her in a welcoming hug. "Hey, doll, you look great!" Carly said.

"Thank you!" Lila exclaimed, happy at the sight of her old friend.

"Are these your new friends from Hockeytown USA?" asked Carly.

"Yes—my new friends!" Lila proudly introduced each one.

"You are very pretty!" Ann said, blushing.

"So are you!" replied Carly.

"Well, look at that! Excuse me, sir, but they only allow goal scorers here!" Jagger Stephen announced, tapping Cullen's shoulder.

"Then why are you here?" Cullen asked, breaking into a smile. The friends shared a hug.

"We should text Aiden our picture!" said McLaren, reaching into his pocket for his phone.

"Chop will be jealous!" said Cullen. "I can't wait to see that kid again!"

"I'm Jagger Stephen," one of the new arrivals told Lila, reaching to shake her hand. Lila gripped his hand perfectly.

"Jagger Stephen and McLaren played outside in Hockeytown USA, last season for Hockey Day," Luke told her.

"That's cool!" Lila responded.

"Yes, it was cool—as in freezing!" Jagger Stephen replied, laughing.

"The players will be out soon. Jason would love to show you the locker room, kids," Carly told everyone.

"We're waiting on the visiting team," McLaren pointed out.

"You mean the losing team," Cullen replied. He was the only one to laugh at his own joke.

"Game's over, and down here sportsmanship picks no side," Carly told him sternly. "Good players inspire themselves. Great players inspire others."

"I like that," Lila said with a smile.

"*You* inspire Jason and me," Carly assured her.

"Me?" Lila asked, surprised.

"You inspire all of us," Avery corrected.

"And me!" Jagger Stephen added, giving Lila's wheelchair a wheelie.

"This is one of my favorite places to come. Look around. After every game, this is what I get to see and hear: regular people doing inspiring actions," Carly shared while pointing to others gathered outside the locker room.

"We like competition and the thrill of a game—especially winning," Jagger Stephen's dad said, coming out of the opposite locker room. "But right here is why we play the game. For the fans."

"Lila! Fast-skatin' Lila!" Jason yelled as he came running to get a hug. "Give me a second, kids. I want to meet everyone else here and talk with them. Then, we can go into the locker room and see the ice too!"

As other players came out of the locker room, they joined Jason with hugs, high-fives, and pictures for the other fans gathered. The friends listened carefully to all the personal, inspirational stories fans shared with the players. This was a common sight outside hockey locker rooms.

There was a former US Marine named Brad who had a wide grin despite being wheelchair- bound with a feeding tube. Backpacks filled with school supplies were handed out to a group of foster youth. Kids from the Bel13ve Foundation were proudly wearing red and white "13" stickers. Players' wives handed out "Cully's Kids" baseball caps to everyone. It was hard to keep a dry eye.

The players knew that the motto from their locker-room wall lived on: "The More Difficult the Victory, the Greater the Happiness in Winning."

"Let's go in!" the players cried.

"Lila, lead the way!" exclaimed Jason.

"Us too?" Jagger Stephen asked his dad.

His dad shrugged his shoulders.

"Of course, you guys come with!" a player replied. "Hockey players leave the game on the ice. After the handshake, we are all teammates in the small circle of hockey."

"I love this!" said Ann.

1

WHEELS UP, SKATES ON

The next day, the friends climbed into in Paisley's van and drove home to Hockeytown USA. They sang songs and shared hockey stories along the way. But, most importantly, they talked about everyone they'd met outside the locker room who had inspired them with motivational words and life stories. The friends daydreamed about creating Hockeytown USA awards for inspirational youth and adults.

"We could make an award for best off-the-ice inspiration," Avery suggested.

"Maybe another for best sportsmanship—like Will Stinson and Tripp showed us!" Luke added.

"It's not every day you see that in youth sports," said Paisley's dad.

"This will be cool!" Ann agreed.

"I like all of this," said Cullen.

"Meeee toooo," replied Blaine.

"Kids who are awesome," Lila said.

"Like us—we are awesome!" added Ann.

All the friends laughed.

"If we can design magnificent Valentine's Day mailboxes, we can design a cool award," Paisley suggested.

"Everyone likes hockey and getting awards—every day and every way!" exclaimed Luke.

"This is so cool," Lila said, eyes sparkling.

"Coooooollllllll," Blaine agreed.

The group dropped Lila off at her home. Her parents greeted the friends and helped Lila out of the van.

"How was it?" her mom asked as Lila's wheels hit the sidewalk.

When Lila paused, her dad cut in, "Everything okay? Did you have a good time?"

Lila smiled. "I had the *best* time. The game was great, and the birthday party was the best ever. But after the game, we met up with Carly and Jason in the locker room!"

Her parents looked surprised.

"It was awesome. We got to see how a lot of different groups gather outside the locker room to meet players and share their life stories," Lila explained.

"How neat!" her mom exclaimed.

"Beyond neat, Mom. It was everyone from a US Marine who was in a wheelchair like me to a group of foster kids getting school supplies, and Cully's Kids was giving out hats! And I saw a lot of Bel13ve Foundation '13' stickers!"

"Everyone has a story to tell, Lila," her dad said.

"Because of that, we decided to make awards for people who inspire us," Lila added.

"Wow. I love these new friends! You are *our* story of inspiration— the queen of grit and determination," her mom told her.

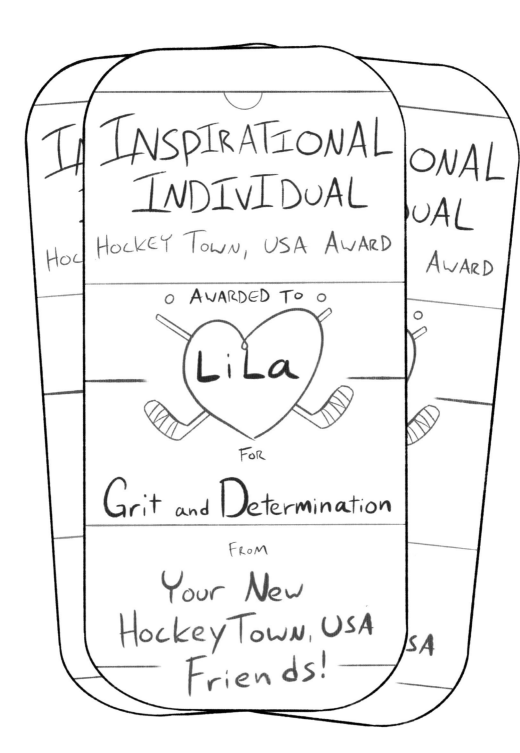

8

JUST BE YOU

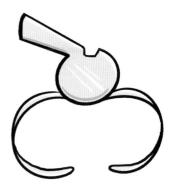

"What a waste of a Saturday," Lila moaned to her parents.

The family was sitting in the local children's specialty hospital, waiting for her doctor visit. "It could be a lot worse. We have it pretty good," Lila's dad stated.

"I haven't been able to skate very much. If I get this surgery, my legs will be weak for months," Lila answered.

"At least you can skate! And you have both legs!" her mom answered.

"Plus a million-dollar smile. We have a lot to be thankful for," her dad replied.

"I hate surgery. I hate missing school. I hate not seeing my friends. I miss out on all the fun stuff. I will miss out on the sledding field trip." Lila began to tear up.

Soon, a bright-and-wide-eyed girl and her mom joined Lila's family in the patient waiting room. The girl, about the same age as Lila, wore glasses and had leopard-printed braces on her trim legs. Lila's mom noticed the girl's mom proudly wearing a cute "Hockey Mom" hoodie.

"I need one of those," Lila's mom blurted out to the new family.

"I can easily arrange for one!" the mom shared while reaching out for a hug.

"I definitely need one—possibly one for every day of the week!" Lila's mom laughed.

The two moms had an instant connection.

"I'm Makenna," the girl introduced herself to Lila.

"Hi…I'm Lila," she answered shyly.

Lila looked at the girl out of the corner of her eye. She noticed her backpack was full of hockey bag tags. She motioned for her mom to see without Makenna noticing. "Just Be You!" really caught Lila's eye.

"That's quite the collection of tags," Lila's mom stated.

"Yes, these are all my favorites. I really like the 'Just Be You!' one," Makenna answered.

"Makenna tell them about yourself," her mom encouraged.

The girls sat in silence. Finally, Makenna broke the ice. "I play hockey and do gymnastics." Makenna beamed.

"I play hockey," Lila mumbled.

"You do? But I skate!" Makenna replied.

"I skate too! See…" Lila stated while showing Makenna a video from her device.

The two girls giggled.

"Wow, that's super cool," Makenna said, showing her mom.

"I was born with cerebral palsy," Lila explained.

"Me too!" Makenna shared.

"You were?" Lila asked.

"I had a wheelchair. Now I wear braces on both legs. You like them?" Makenna asked pulling up her skirt to show off the leopard print.

"Why are you here on a Saturday?" Lila asked Makenna.

"I don't want to be here. But I'm supposed to have surgery to help my nerves in my back and legs," Makenna answered like a mini physician.

"What? Wait? For real? Me too!" Lila exclaimed.

Suddenly, the girls both noticed their matching pink polished nails. They indeed had much in common.

"From hockey to special needs, we are blessed to meet you. We need a friend or three being here!" Lila's mom reached out to Makenna's mom for a second hug.

"Totally agree," the mom responded.

"Lila—Lila, the doctor is ready," the nurse announced.

"I'll give Makenna's mom my cell number," her mom assured her.

"I've got your back," Makenna said to Lila.

"Me too!" Lila laughed.

"Just be you!" Makenna yelled.

At school on Monday, the friends gathered around Miss Marvin to share their idea of honoring people who motivate them.

"We want to start an award for inspirational hockey winners, on and off the ice," Cullen explained.

"We want to recognize that everyone has a story to share," Avery added.

"And we can help share those stories," Luke chimed in.

"Yeesssss weeeee cannnn," Blaine stated as he sat down by Lila.

"I know at least two people who should get awards," Lila said excitedly. "One is my friend Tripp, who invented Le-Glue, and the other is my new friend Makenna, who was born with cerebral palsy just like me. She plays hockey and does gymnastics and only uses braces to walk!"

"Wow…that'sss sssomething!" Blaine exclaimed.

"I love your motivation and idea," Miss Marvin said enthusiastically.

"We should announce the awards on Valentine's Day and grow our small-town tradition beyond Hockeytown USA," Avery suggested.

"A whole lotta heart! We could send a Valentine to every award nominee," Lila offered.

"Yeessssss!" Blaine cheered.

"Let's do it!" said Ann.

"We can recognize all the great kids from arena to arena and coast to coast," Miss Marvin agreed.

"Team to team!" Cullen added.

"Wheels up!" Lila said.

"Skates on!" her friends all chimed in.

ASK THE OFFICIALS

Important Words to Learn

Bel13ve Foundation:	The Jack Jablonski BEL13VE in Miracles Foundation is a charitable organization created to support spinal cord injury recovery. The foundation is driven to advance medical research and innovative treatments that are achieving victories over paralysis.
Brainstormed:	Produced an idea or way of solving a problem by holding a spontaneous group discussion.
Burlap Baker:	A terrific baker located in Logan, Iowa.
Cross-country skiing:	A form of ski touring in which participants propel themselves across snow-covered terrain using skis and poles.

Cully's Kids: Cullen Children's Foundation provides financial resources to organizations that support children's healthcare needs with an emphasis on cancer. The foundation is led by Bridget and Matt Cullen.

Determination: Firmness of purpose; resoluteness.

Great One: The nickname of Wayne Douglas Gretzky, a Canadian former professional ice hockey player and former head coach. He played twenty-one seasons in the National Hockey League (NHL) for four teams from 1979 to 1999.

Humiliating: Causing someone to feel ashamed and foolish by injuring their dignity and self-respect.

Inspirational: Providing or showing creative or spiritual ideas.

Le-Glue: A product created by Tripp Phillips when he was thirteen. He lives in Georgia with his mom and dad, his sister Allee, and their dog, Skippy. During the cold month of December 2014, Tripp entered the International Torrance Legacy Creativity

Awards competition. In order to win the competition, Tripp had to come up with an idea for a new product, something that had never been made before, something that kids and some grown-ups alike really needed. Le-Glue won the Inventions: Toys and Games category.

Papier-mâché: The traditional method of making papier-mâché adhesive is to use a mixture of water and flour or other starch, mixed to the consistency of heavy cream. Other adhesives can be used if thinned to a similar texture.

Rival: A person or thing competing with another for the same objective or for superiority in the same field of activity.

US Marine: A member of the United States Marine Corps, also referred to as the United States Marines or US Marines, which is a branch of the United States Armed Forces responsible for conducting expeditionary and amphibious operations with the United States Navy as well as the Army and Air Force.

MEET JAYNE

Jayne J. Jones Beehler wears many helmets, including hockey sister, college professor, lawyer, author, wife, mother, advocate for children with disabilities, and lifelong hockey fan. She's also a former live-in nanny who can never have enough children or chaos around her. Jayne resides in Florida with her husband, a hockey coach and former goalie. Every night, there's a game on their TV! Together, they founded a chaperone travel nonprofit organization to ensure that individuals with developmental disabilities can travel independently.

www.officialadventures.org

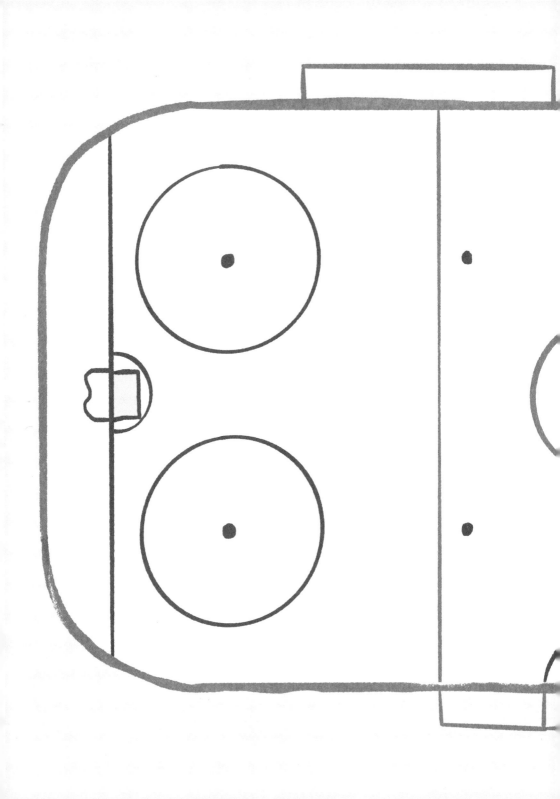